Milton's
Suitcase
Adventure

written by
Diane Distefano

illustrated by
Manny Pantoja

LUMINARE PRESS
WWW.LUMINAREPRESS.COM

Luminare Press
442 Charnelton St.
Eugene, OR 97401
www.luminarepress.com

LCCN: 2022922130
ISBN: 979-8-88679-187-7

To Ava and Alice,
who have a whole world
yet to explore.

Milton the dog loved to nap—and a lot!

He snoozed day and night—
in any old spot!

He slept on
old blankets,

on beds—
and below...

...in tight nooks,

hidden crannies—

any place he could stow.

Anytime, anyplace,
it didn't matter where...

Until one day his snooze
took him far, far away...

...when he napped in a suitcase that belonged to Aunt Kay!

Across lands and oceans,
places far and wide...

...Milton was off on a big adventure,
and he hadn't even tried!

He awoke when they landed—in Paris.

"Where am I?"

He worried and felt bad.
Milton wanted to cry.

But Aunt Kay knew
what mattered
and made a
quick call.

Told the family all was well...

...then rode them off to the mall.

She bought a fancy collar and leash, just the same...

...a spa treatment,
custom jacket, and
a beret with his name.

Then Milton set out to explore all things French...

...taking on Paris, even making new friends!

Napping in museums, painting, trying new cheese...

...snoozing in parks, near statues and leaves.

On his last day in Paris,
it started to rain!
Milton ran for cover and
hopped on a train.

His trip nearly over,
yet so much to explore,
he thought he had time
to do just a bit more.

Milton awoke with a start
and was filled with dismay.

He'd snoozed on the Métro
and slept the whole day!

Worse yet, he was late for his
flight with Aunt Kay!

Milton grabbed his map and
knew what to do next:
asked in his best French to
please send out a text.

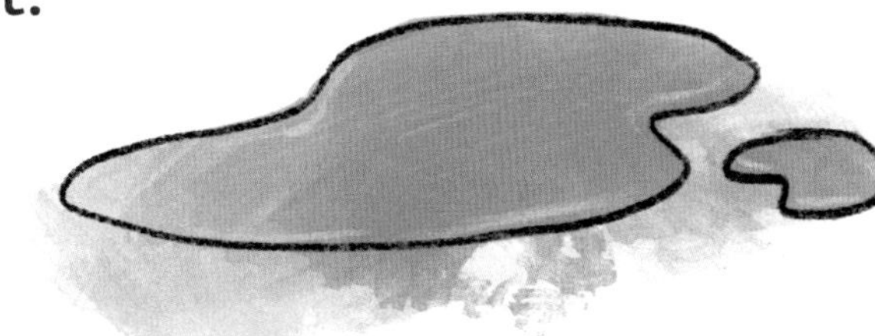

And then to the rescue,
his friends rushed to help.

Caught his plane just in time—
Milton let out a yelp!

Then the doorbell rang out!
Milton was finally back home...

...with mustache,

beret, baguette—

and new phone!

These days he's happy
sharing all the new skills
he learned on his trip—
between all the thrills.

Milton learned he loves baking
and painting and such.

He doesn't fear trying
new things quite as much.

With a new zest for life and a world
to explore, he can zipline in China,
surf Hawaii's North Shore!

Milton's making big plans
as he dreams every day...

...of his next new adventure
with his best pal, Aunt Kay.

About the Author

Diane Distefano is an award-winning journalist and writer at the University of California San Diego. A mother of two and proud nana to Ava and Alice, her passions include crafting, gardening, and travel. In her teens, Diane became an avid reader, particularly drawn to offbeat humor and unpredictable story lines in films and print; both continue to heavily influence her writing. A California native, she lives in San Diego with husband, Chris, and one very special pup. Milton is based on their snoozy, curious, snaggle-toothed rescue of the same name. **www.dianedistefano.com**

About the Artist

Manny Pantoja is an illustrator, painter, and graphic designer. His love of art and sense of wanderlust has taken him all over the world. Manny resides in California where he enjoys plein air painting and urban adventuring. **www.mannypantoja.com**

Many thanks...

To Chris, who laughed in all the right places and offered a boatload of encouraging words—especially when I got stuck.

To Manny, who made our collaboration as much fun as I'd hoped and brought Milton to life with his incredible artistry. Out of lockdown, we birthed a book!

To Vince and Lauren, for teaching me the importance of story time and those sticky-fingered lessons only parenthood can reveal. Your loving support has been invaluable.

To Patty, who checked my French, and to Ava, for giving me a four-year-old's perspective.

To my parents, for making sure that books, music, and humor were ever-present in our household. Thank you for the room to be creative.

To my friends, colleagues, and family members, for your assistance and enthusiasm.

And, of course, thanks to Milton, who inspires me to be a better human every day.

Made in the USA
Las Vegas, NV
31 May 2023